ONE LUCKY DOG

WRITTEN BY LIBBY BAGBY
AND JAN CARMICHAEL

ILLUSTRATED BY
HEIDI CARR HARRIS

DEDICATION

To Madelyn Seale and Riley Aiken, my grand niece and nephew--I hope someday you will have the opportunity to earn the companionship, love, and respect of a pet.--LB

To Krista and Rebekah, my beautiful daughters--the loves of my life.--Mom (JC)

ACKNOWLEDGEMENTS

Thanks to all of those who helped with this book--my coauthor Jan Carmichael for helping me realize my dream of writing a second children's book, our editors, Penelope Schwartz and Lisa Kline, and my sister Patricia and grand nephew Riley for being co-editors. Thanks also to my special friend JoAn Stout, a passionate writer, for her marvelous suggestions. Many thanks, too, go out to all my other family members and friends Becky and Una, to Mrs. Emily March's first grade class and to Mrs. Neely Barham's second grade class at Lyle Creek Elementary in Hickory, NC. Most of all thanks to my husband Rick, who is my strength.--LB

A huge thank you to everyone who has been with me through this "first book journey"--my coauthor, Libby Bagby, who made me realize that writing my first book did not need to wait until I retired and had faith in me all along the way, my family and friends, who supported me in each phase of this journey, the students and teachers at Union Hill Elementary School, who allowed me to share the Lucky books with them as we have grown to know and love Libby and Lucky, and to my dog Lucky, who has inspired me to begin writing because of his rescue story and companionship for the last 15 years.--JC

This book is a work of fiction. People, places, events, and situations are the product of the authors' imaginations. Any resemblance to actual persons, living or dead, or historical events, is purely coincidental.

© Libby Bagby and Jan Carmichael. All rights reserved. No part of this book may be reproduced, stored in a retrieval system, or transmitted by any means without the written permission of the authors. ISBN # 978-1-4675-5946-1

Printed in Asheboro, NC by PIP Printing.

On a clear and crisp January night
With the full moon shining ever so bright
And my keen nose close to the ground to help,
I sniff and sniff. "Yippee! Raccoon!" I yelp!
"Yo, yo, yo and away I go!"
"Yo, yo, yo and away I go!"

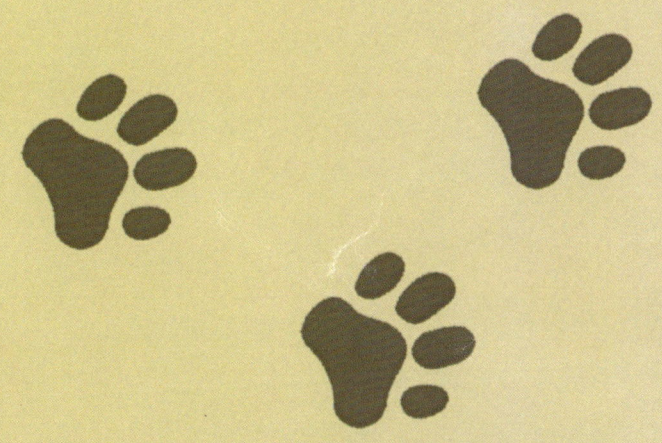

I trap him in a hollow maple tree.
And that mangy, black-eyed rascal bites me.
Off in a flash into a stream he goes,
I follow him, and he jumps on my nose!
"Yo, yo, yo and away we go!"
"Yo, yo, yo and away we go!"

He sprints from the stream with me on his trail.
Bright lights blind me--into the air I sail.
A car has just hit me, what will I do?
My legs hurt so badly, will I pull through?
"Yo, yo, yo how I wish I could go!"
"Yo, yo, yo how I wish I could go!"

3

I drift off to sleep, afraid and alone.
I wake up and all I can do is groan.
I watch cars race by, and none of them stop.
I try to bark, but my head wants to drop.
"Yo, yo, yo how I wish I could go!"
"Yo, yo, yo how I wish I could go!"

4

To my surprise, kind strangers stop my way.
Blankets surround me--in their truck I stay.
They rush me to town where there is a vet.
The doctor says, "His hind legs must be set."
"Yo, yo, yo how I wish I could go!"
"Yo, yo, yo how I wish I could go!"

5

I sleep and rest as days slowly pass by.
When will I walk or run or want to try?
My kind rescuer comes to visit me.
Seeing him again fills my heart with glee.
"Yo, yo, yo and away we go!"
"Yo, yo, yo and away we go!"

6

Happily riding with wind in my face,
I wonder--are we going to his place?
Hoping this would be my forever home
With a new, rolling countryside to roam.
"Yo, yo, yo and away we go!"
"Yo, yo, yo and away we go!"

7

I love my new home--it is so cozy.
My future looks bright--some call it rosy.
Is that the scent of a dog in the air?
Oh! I can't wait for my legs to repair!
"Yo, yo, yo and away we'll go!"
"Yo, yo, yo and away we'll go!"

8

Ever so slowly I begin to move.
After awhile I am into the groove.
My new furry friend and I bark and play.
And I can romp and run with him today!
"Yo, yo, yo and away we go!"
"Yo, yo, yo and away we go!"

Happy to be with my new family,
I am one lucky dog--Don't you agree?
It was a joyful day when I was found.
They renamed me *Lucky*—I'm one blessed hound.
"Yo, yo, yo and away I go!"
"Yo, yo, yo and away I go!"

About Lucky

On January 25, 2002, as I was driving home from my job, I saw a black dog lying by the roadside on Highway 89 between Mt. Airy and Low Gap, NC. Since he was not moving, I worried that he was dead. But as my car passed him, I sensed movement out of my peripheral vision and glanced in the rearview mirror to discover that he had raised his head and was staring in my car's direction. With the help of three other good Samaritans and my husband Rick, we rescued the dog from this busy country road.

At the veterinarian's office, we discovered he had broken two back legs, was severely dehydrated, and was having trouble breathing since his lungs had filled with fluid. The prognosis was not encouraging. After a few days he rebounded, and we brought him home to join our already-large canine family shown right.

We knew that "Lucky" was the only name that was appropriate for this dog since he had survived such serious injuries. We felt that he was lucky, too, that we adopted him since we had five other dogs at home at that time. Sadly, these dogs are all gone.

Dogs from L to R are Sillie, Millie, Buddy, Rusty & Tyler

At a follow-up visit to the vet's, we learned that his breed was a Plott Hound and that North Carolina officially recognized it as our state dog in 1989. Rescuing Lucky has expanded our lives in so many ways that Rick and I now realize we were truly the *lucky* ones.

Lucky, now 12 years old, spends his days sunning in our backyard, relaxing on the deck, and sleeping. He also enjoys his two daily walks accompanied by our two newest rescues--Rolo, our Chocolate Lab, and Foxxy, a Pomeranian-Chow mix. But, most of all he likes hitting the road to share about the Plott breed with people throughout North Carolina. To date, Lucky has done his part in presentations to almost 14,000 children and adults. In five years, we have presented "Staying on Track with *Lucky's Plott*" at schools, public libraries, museums, and book festivals in over 40 of North Carolina's 100 counties. If you would like more information on the Plott breed, Lucky's books, or to schedule a presentation, just visit our website at www.luckysplott.com and click on the email link. We promise our presentations are one "howling" good time for all! "Yo, yo, yo and *plotting* we go!"

About The Authors—Two *Lucky* Women

Tar Heel born and raised, Libby Bagby has always loved dogs and has had one by her side since she was a child. Over the years, she and her husband Rick have shared their home with twelve canines. However, when they rescued a black brindle dog in 2002, it changed the *plot* of their lives forever.

Retiring as a high school educator, Libby anticipated spending her days reading, gardening, traveling, and bicycling. Those plans were placed on hold when she discovered the dog they rescued was a Plott Hound--North Carolina's State Dog. Now her days at their Roaring Gap home are filled with researching, interviewing, writing, or traveling North Carolina with Lucky teaching about this courageous hunting breed, sharing the rewards of animal rescue, and encouraging children to read.

Jan Carmichael has always lived in the Jamestown area of North Carolina, except for those wonderful four years in Boone as a student at Appalachian State University. She grew up with many rescue dogs in her life just as her daughters, Krista and Rebekah, have grown up with their current rescues, Lucky and Tigger.

As a 27 year teaching veteran, she has taught in elementary schools in the Guilford County School System as a classroom teacher, reading specialist and currently as an English as a Second Language teacher. Her plans were to begin writing children's books when she retired, but the timing of that changed when she met Libby and Lucky at a book signing. As with many teachers, she has her own collection of children's books and many of them are dog stories, so when she first began this journey with Libby and Lucky she realized this was just not another dog book to add to her collection. Learning and writing about the Plott Hound has definitely changed the *plot* of her life, too.

About the Illustrator

Heidi Carr Harris grew up in rural Northwestern North Carolina. Her artistic talents were apparent at a very young age and were encouraged through the years. Her passion for animals inspired her work and many of her pieces feature horses and/or dogs. She has won ribbons for her acrylic paintings, but she also enjoys working with a variety of other media such as charcoal, watercolor, pastels, and graphite. She earned a degree in Advertising and Graphic Design at Surry Community College in 2009. She currently lives with her husband in the foothills of North Carolina, and, together, they own three horses, two Miniature Dachshunds, and a Golden Labrador Retriever.